MORE MOLE STORIES
and Little Gopher, Too

LORE SEGAL

Pictures by SERGIO RUZZIER

Frances Foster Books • Farrar, Straus and Giroux • New York

Distributed in Canada by Douglas & McIntyre Ltd.
Color separations by Chroma Graphics PTE Ltd.
Printed and bound in the United States of America by Berryville Graphics
Designed by Barbara Grzeslo
First edition, 2005
1   3   5   7   9   10   8   6   4   2

www.fsgkidsbooks.com

Library of Congress Cataloging-in-Publication Data
Segal, Lore Groszmann.
    More Mole stories and Little Gopher, too / Lore Segal ; pictures by Sergio
Ruzzier.— 1st ed.
        p.   cm.
    Contents: Mole and the Thursday cookie — Mole and Little Gopher, or
yours plus mine equals mine — Mole and the whole bag of pretzels — When
Grandmother Mole got on the telephone.
    ISBN-13: 978-0-374-35026-0
    ISBN-10: 0-374-35026-4
    [1. Moles (Animals)—Fiction.   2. Gophers—Fiction.   3. Grandmothers—
Fiction.]   I. Ruzzier, Sergio, ill.   II. Title.

PZ7.S4527M1 2005
[Fic]—dc22

                                                              2003064270

To Benjamin and Isaiah again
—L.S.

For Elena, Alessandra, and Marta
—S.R.

MOLE AND THE THURSDAY COOKIE
Chapter 1

Once there was a Mole. He lived with his Grandmother Mole in a hole in the forest, and they would have been perfectly happy if only Mole had saved his chocolate chip cookies to eat after supper.

Now you may or may not know this, but moles are insectivores and ants are insects, so moles have to finish up the ants on their plate before they get to eat their cookies.

One day Grandmother Mole said, "I've brought you some cookies in a bag to have with your milk."

"Can I put the bag next to my plate," asked Mole, "just to look at?"

"Just to look. Promise?" Grandmother asked him.

"I promise," said Mole.

Mole put the bag next to his plate and looked at it. But you know how it is when you're looking at a bag: you need to look inside. Mole looked inside the bag and there were *two* chocolate chip cookies!

Mole looked at his plate. There were two ants, and they were looking at him.

"Run away! Scoot!" Mole told them.

"Gee! Thanks a lot!" the ants said.

Mole was watching the ants running away, so he didn't notice that his paw had somehow got inside the bag and was feeling the cookies up and down. A piece broke off and got into his mouth. Now *this* piece of cookie—the one that got into Mole's mouth—had a chip of chocolate in it, and you know how it is when your mouth gets chocolate in it. It wants *more* chocolate. There was Mole all of a sudden with the whole chocolate chip cookie inside his mouth!

When he saw his Grandmother Mole coming with the milk, he quickly put the second cookie in his mouth, where there really wasn't even room for it.

Grandmother Mole saw the empty plate and said, "Now you can have your chocolate chip cookies."

Chapter 2

She opened the bag, and there wasn't a crumb left!

"You didn't keep your promise," said Mole's Grandmother Mole. "From now on, you get one cookie once a week. Every Thursday you can have a chocolate chip cookie, but only one."

"What day is it today?" Mole asked his Grandmother Mole.

"Thursday," she said, "and you've had your cookie."

Mole went to sleep and when he woke up it was Friday.

"Eat your ants," said his Grandmother Mole.

Mole went to sleep again and woke and it was Saturday.

Mole asked Grandmother Mole when it was going to be Thursday, and there was still Sunday, Monday, Tuesday, and Wednesday to go.

On Wednesday Grandmother Mole said, "When you wake up tomorrow it will be Thursday, and you can have your chocolate chip cookie. But only just one!"

The next day Mole woke and was sad. "I can't have my chocolate chip cookie," he said.

"Yes you can," said his Grandmother Mole.

"But I can't," said Mole. "I dreamed that it was Thursday and I ate it."

"Well," Grandmother Mole said to him, "because you are an

honest Mole, you get to have two chocolate chip cookies. You get to have the cookie you dreamed and you get to eat your Thursday cookie. Only just this one Thursday."

MOLE AND LITTLE GOPHER
or Yours Plus Mine Equals Mine

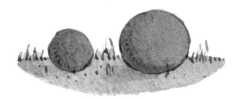

Once there was a Mole. He had a Grandmother, and they would have lived happily together if only he hadn't kept saying **"Mine!"** and **"I want it!"**

On Tuesday, when Grandmother Gopher brought Little Gopher to play, Mole gave Little Gopher his best purple ball to play with.

Grandmother Gopher said, "Aren't you a nice Mole!"

But that's when Mole grabbed the red ball that Little Gopher had brought with him.

Little Gopher said, **"That's mine!"** and sat down on the floor and cried.

Grandmother Mole told Mole, "Share nicely!"

And Grandmother Gopher told Little Gopher, "You play with Mole's purple ball and let Mole play with your red ball."

But Mole grabbed his purple ball out of Little Gopher's paws.

Now Little Gopher didn't have his own red ball and he didn't have Mole's purple ball either. He howled.

Grandmother Mole said, "Give him back his red ball. It's his."

Mole said, **"But I want it."**

"Then let him play with your purple ball," said Grandmother Mole.

Mole said, **"It's mine."**

Grandmother Mole got up, took the red ball away from Mole, and gave it back to Little Gopher, who stopped howling. Then she took Mole's purple ball away from him, and Mole lay down on the floor and cried so loudly Grandmother Mole said, "Oh for goodness' sake!" and gave it back to him. She said, "Be nice to each other!"

"Look how nicely they're playing," Grandmother Gopher said to Grandmother Mole.

Mole was rolling his purple ball to Little Gopher and Little Gopher was rolling his red ball to Mole, who picked it up and threw it.

"Careful," said Grandmother Gopher.

Grandmother Mole said, "No throwing indoors."

Mole said, **"But I want to."** He picked up his purple ball and threw it. It hit Little Gopher in the head.

"You hit my Little Gopher in the head," hollered Grandmother Gopher. "You are a bad Mole!"

"No he's *not*!" shouted Grandmother Mole. "He's not bad! He is my own Mole, and it so happens he is *good*!" But to her Mole she said, "If you throw that ball again, I'm going to take it away, and this time I won't give it back."

Mole threw it again.

Grandmother Mole got up and said, "Give me that ball."

But Mole ran and grabbed Little Gopher's red ball and threw it out the window!

"Your Mole," hollered Grandmother Gopher, "has thrown *my* Little Gopher's own red ball out the window!"

Little Gopher, who thought this was fun, ran and threw Mole's purple ball out the window.

"And *your* Little Gopher," shouted Grandmother Mole, "has thrown *my* Mole's best purple ball out the window!"

"Yes," yelled Grandmother Gopher, "but he's only a *baby*! Come!" she said to Little Gopher. "We're going home."

But Little Gopher was having fun, what with the red ball and the purple ball and rolling them and throwing them out the window. He said, **"I don't want to!"** and lay down on his back and howled.

"Now look what you've done!" Grandmother Mole hollered, and Mole sat down and cried.

Such a to-do, what with Grandmother Mole and Grandmother Gopher standing and yelling and hollering, and Mole and Little Gopher sitting and lying and howling and crying!

And so then they had their tea . . .

. . . and drank their milk. Grandmother Mole brought out the chocolate-covered ants.

At four o'clock Grandmother Gopher said, "Goodbye," and Little Gopher waved, and everybody said, "See you next Tuesday."

MOLE AND THE WHOLE BAG OF PRETZELS

Once there was a Mole who lived with his Grandmother Mole in a hole in the forest.

Now you may or may not know this, but moles love picnics. Grandmother Mole spread a blanket and took out the pretzels, and what did Mole do? He snatched the whole bag and ran away with it.

"You come back here," cried Grandmother Mole. "What do you want with a whole bag of pretzels? You can only eat one at a time."

"I can eat one after the other," said Mole.

Grandmother Mole said, "I have an idea: you can take two pretzels, one in one paw to eat right away and another to hold in your other paw to eat after that."

"I can't do that," said Mole, "because in one paw I've got the pretzel I'm going to eat right away and in my other paw I'm holding the bag."

"But you have to share!" cried his Grandmother. "You're not the only mole in the world who loves pretzels. They're salty and they crunch and I want some too."

But Mole did not give the bag of pretzels back.

Grandmother Mole said, "How about putting half the pretzels in this dish for me, and you can have the other half. Isn't that a good idea?"

"No," said Mole, "because I want the whole bag."

"You aren't being a very nice Mole today," said his Grandmother Mole.

"I know," said Mole.

Mole was trying to think of an idea that could make him give back that bag of pretzels, and he couldn't.

Mole said, "*I* have an idea. I'll give *you* two pretzels, one to hold in one paw to eat now, and one for your other paw to eat after. How would you like that?"

"I would like you to give the bag back," said Grandmother Mole, "which you are not going to do, right?"

"You're right," said Mole. "But after you finish your two pretzels, I will give you two more, and after that I'll give you one more, but only just one."

"Well, you're not really such a bad Mole!" said his Grandmother Mole. "Come here and I'll give you a hug."

WHEN GRANDMOTHER MOLE
GOT ON THE TELEPHONE

Once there was a Mole who lived with his Grandmother, and they got on well enough except when Grandmother Mole got talking on the Telephone.

There was that Telephone ringing, ringing.

Grandmother Mole picked up the Telephone, sat down in her rocking chair, and said, "Fine, and how are you feeling?"

Who was Grandmother Mole talking to? High-Nose the Weasel, or Swashbuckle Tail the Red Squirrel, or Chittering Brown Squirrel? Could it be Uncle Velvet Mole or Little Gopher's Grandmother Gopher?

The one Grandmother Mole was *not* talking to was Mole. Grandmother Mole didn't ask Mole how *he* was feeling!

Mole said, "I am feeling hungry and I need a pretzel."

"In a minute," Grandmother Mole said, and went on talking on the Telephone.

Mole said, "And I can't find my glasses!"

Grandmother Mole said, "Where did you put them?" and leaned back in her rocking chair and cozied in, talking and smiling, but not at Mole. Grandmother Mole wasn't so much as *looking* at Mole.

"Grandmother Mole, look at me standing on my head! Hey, Grandmother Mole! Look!"

Grandmother Mole waved him away with her paw.

"I want a chocolate chip cookie!" Mole said.

But Grandmother Mole went on talking on the Telephone.

And talking and talking.

Grandmother Mole had forgotten about Mole. Mole began to run around in circles yelling, "Awooo!"

"Aweee!" yelled Grandmother Mole. Mole was climbing up the back of her rocking chair so that Grandmother Mole's two hind paws went up in the air.

"I've got to go," she told the Telephone. "Talk to you later!" and she put the Telephone down, and sighed. "Oh for goodness' sake!"

Mole knew that she was talking to *him*.

She said, "Why won't you let your poor old Grandmother Mole have a nice talk on the Telephone?"

Then she kissed him on his nose. "You may or may not know this," she told him, "but grandmothers don't love their friends the weasels, the squirrels, the gophers, and all the uncles in the world one half as much as they always love their own dear Mole. So," she said, "let's see you stand on your head."